WHERE WE BELONG

SAMIKHYA PATRA

Made with ♥ on the Notion Press Platform
www.notionpress.com

to my parents, sister, dog and late grandfather; family that
matter the most.

Contents

Preface

Writing this book has been a journey of growth, both creatively and personally. When I first began crafting the story of Satya and her transformative experiences, I had no idea how deeply it would come to reflect some of my own challenges, dreams, and hopes. Satya's story emerged from a place of longing—a longing to explore themes that resonate with many of us: identity, family, tradition, and the power of self-belief. Through her, I wanted to address the complexities of life's choices and the emotional crossroads we often find ourselves at, especially when it comes to family and legacy.

I myself lost my grandparents when I was 5 or 6. I always wanted to spend more time with them and always wished that I could know them better. Satya's story became an exploration of those themes. Through her eyes, I was able to express the joys and pains of reconciling with one's roots, navigating the tensions between the past and the present, and ultimately finding strength in connection.

As I developed Satya's character, she grew into more than just a protagonist. She became a vessel for ideas that I had struggled with myself. Her deep connection to her grandfather, her initial doubts about her place in the world, and her slow but determined rise to a position of inner strength are reflections of struggles that many of us experience. Through her, I wanted to explore how the older generations influence who we are, even long after they're gone, and how our personal histories can either anchor us or free us, depending on how we choose to interpret them.

In writing this book, one of the major challenges I faced was balancing the weight of tradition with the demands of modern life. I didn't want the story to be a simple tale of nostalgia or longing for the "good old days." Instead, I wanted to highlight how Satya's growth isn't just about reconnecting with her family's past, but also about finding her own path. Her family's fractured state and the emotional wounds that come with it are not healed by simple reconnections but by her strength to move forward and embrace her own role in shaping their future. This mirrors my belief that while family can provide a foundation, it's our individual choices that ultimately define us.

Writing this book was also a personal test. There were many moments when I wasn't sure if I could do justice to the story I wanted to tell. There were periods of doubt—doubt about whether I was capturing Satya's emotional depth accurately, doubt about whether readers would find her journey relatable, and even doubt about whether I could finish the project at all. But each time I returned to the manuscript, I found new reasons to keep going. Satya's perseverance became my own. Her resilience reminded me of the importance of pushing forward even when the end seems far off.

This book is also a reflection of my own evolving understanding of family. Through Satya's story, I was able to revisit some of my own memories and reconsider the value of those connections that once seemed distant or broken. The more I wrote, the more I realized how much of our strength comes from our relationships with others. And even when those relationships are strained or fractured, there's always a possibility of renewal. In the end, this story is about that possibility—the hope that even in the most difficult circumstances, there's always a path forward, a way to find reconciliation and growth.

I hope that readers of this book will find something of themselves in Satya's journey. Whether it's her struggles with identity, her evolving relationship with her family, or her quiet moments of introspection, I believe that her experiences are universal. Each of us faces challenges, and each of us must make decisions about how we relate to the people who have shaped our lives. Through Satya, I hope readers will see that while the past is important, it does not define us; what matters is how we move forward with the lessons we've learned.

Lastly, this book is dedicated to those who have ever doubted their place in the world. Satya's journey is one of self-discovery, but it's also a testament to the power of belief—belief in oneself and in the possibilities that life offers. I believe that each of us has a story to tell, a role to play in the world, and that, like Satya, we can find our strength in the most unexpected places. Writing this book has been a humbling experience, and I'm grateful to everyone who encouraged me to see it through.

In closing, I invite you, the reader, to walk with Satya through her struggles, her moments of doubt, and her eventual triumphs. As you turn the pages, I hope that you, too, find inspiration in her journey and are reminded of the power of resilience, family, and the indomitable human spirit.

Acknowledgements

This work represents my personal journey and I owe it entirely to my own efforts and dedication. From the conception of the story to the final draft, every word and idea comes from the heart.

also special thanks to google, chatgpt and my dictionary for helping me correct my errors and find the right words;)

to the readers- thank you for stepping into this world i created. Your attention is my greatest reward.

Prologue

In the dim light of dawn, the old house stood still, its walls a silent witness to the passage of time. It was a house that had once been alive with laughter, bustling with the sounds of children playing in the courtyard, elders speaking of days gone by, and the hum of everyday life that spun around the heart of the family that called it home. Now, its wooden beams creaked with age, and the once-vibrant rooms sat in a solemn quiet, as if waiting for something—or someone—to bring life back into them.

This house had seen generations pass through its doors. It had seen families grow and then scatter, like seeds carried by the wind to distant lands, leaving behind memories like whispers carried on a breeze. In those early years, it was a place of togetherness, where tradition held the family close, and no one dared to think of a future without one another. But time has a way of loosening even the tightest bonds, and slowly, the family that had once filled this home began to drift apart. Each new generation brought with it new ambitions, new dreams, and new distances—emotional and physical—that pulled them away from the house that had once been their anchor.

Among all those who had left, there was one who never truly let go of the place, even when her life carried her far from it. Satya had grown up with the stories of this house, with the tales of her grandfather's wisdom, his strength, and the values he had instilled in every member of their family. For her, the house had always been more than just a building—it was a symbol of the legacy her grandfather had left behind, a legacy that had shaped who she was and who she would become. Though she had been away for years, building her own life in a world that often felt so different from the one she'd known in her childhood, Satya could never quite shake the feeling that she belonged here, in this place where it all began.

Her grandfather had always been the heart of the family. His steady presence, his quiet strength, and his unwavering belief in family values were the foundation upon which generations stood. To him, family was not just a bond of blood but a responsibility, a sacred duty to carry forward the traditions and values that had been passed down through time. Satya had admired him deeply, though as a child she had not always understood the weight of his words or the wisdom behind his actions. But now, as she stood at the edge of her own life, making decisions that would shape her future, she found herself returning to his teachings time and again.

It was her grandfather who had taught her the importance of patience and resilience. He was quiet and wise. She could not spend a lot of time with him but his memories remained with her.

But now, as Satya stood on the cusp of a new chapter in her life, she knew it was time to return. Time to honor the legacy her grandfather had left behind. The house, once filled with life and love, now stood waiting, as if it knew that it, too, needed healing. Satya felt a pull, a call to bring her family back together, to revive the spirit of unity that had once defined them. She wasn't sure if it was possible—too much time had passed, too many wounds had festered in the silence between them—but she knew she had to try.

The journey ahead would not be easy. There were still unresolved tensions, old grievances, and the inevitable changes that time brings to every family. But Satya believed in the strength of the roots her grandfather had planted. She believed in the power of family, in the connections that could withstand even the harshest storms. She had spent years searching for her place in the world, but now she realized that the answers had been here all along, waiting for her to come home.

As she walked through the familiar halls of the old house, memories flooded back—of summers spent under the shade of the great banyan tree, of evenings listening to her grandfather's stories, and of the love that had always, despite everything, held them together. She could feel the weight of those memories now, but instead of dragging her down, they lifted her. This was her home, her family, and she was ready to step into the role her grandfather had once held, to be the one who would bring them back together.

In this house, where the past and present intertwined, Satya knew she would find the strength to move forward. She would rebuild the bonds that had frayed over time. She would honor the legacy her grandfather had left her and, in doing so, create a future that would keep their family's roots strong, even as their branches continued to grow.

The path ahead was uncertain, but Satya was ready to walk it. She was ready to find her place, to build her future on the foundation of her past. And as she sat in her grandfather's favorite chair, feeling the weight of his presence even now, she knew she wasn't alone. The spirit of family, of love, and of resilience was with her, guiding her every step.

CHAPTER ONE

THE RETURN

Satya always thought success would feel like freedom, but standing at the doorstep of her grandparents' abandoned home, she realized it was the past that held the key to her future.

"Roshan, are you sure this is the place?" It was absolutely her idea to come back to her hometown, to her ancestral house. It was a beautiful old bungalow with an aesthetic green backyard full of bougainvillea and butterflies. Satya only had a few pictorial memories left with her.

She had memories of the house, but they were like whispers in a storm—faint, fragmented, and slipping further away with each passing year. She couldn't recall much. A young lady, who was at the peak of her career, living a dreamy, luxurious, and independent life as a fashion designer with her own label abroad, Satya had nothing but a sense of emotional nostalgia to bring her back. This young girl had spent most of her life reading, studying, and trying to prove that she was the best, that she was absolutely perfect.

Satya could never become number one in school, but she won in life. Her hopes and dreams never deceived her. Her parents weren't wealthy enough to afford the best European education for her, so she decided to complete her bachelor's degree here in India. By the time she got her own pay check and was independent enough to pay her own bills, she left.

"Madam, it was your idea and plan to come back to this place. How am I supposed to know if this is the place or not?" said Satya's stylist and assistant, Roshan, in a quirky way. He had been a part of almost her entire journey and was like her brother, a part of her family.

The reason Satya had returned to this house was because of the sense of emptiness and detachment from family and values. Of course, she was in touch and close with her mom, dad, and her brother, but what about the big joint family they had when she was a young child? Why did everyone part ways? Why did everyone become so distant?

Such questions hit her all of a sudden after years of living alone, focused solely on her career. She had her own label, Pravah, which means "flow" in Hindi—just like how life is a flow of ever-changing moments, emotions, and untold stories, weaving together the threads of our past, present, and future. With every design, she aimed to capture this movement—a reminder that nothing stays the same, yet everything is connected.

She wanted to bring her designs back to India and stay more in touch with the culture and the place where she had established her business.

"Madam, I understand that this place is absolutely stunning, with its rustic charm and vintage elegance, but I'd suggest we head inside so we can unpack your collection and start setting up the space properly," said Roshan. His eye for detail was impeccable—always noticing the way textures played with light or how a space could breathe life into a design.

As Satya stepped inside, there were cobwebs and layers of dust everywhere. It seemed as if the interior had never been cleaned, even though there were gardeners, maids, and cleaners who took care of the exterior. No one lived there, so it was a wonder why the house was being maintained at all.

Nevertheless, Satya was ready to turn this old, unswept, and grimy place into her very own magical and comforting sanctuary. There were papers, frames, random cupboards, and whatnot scattered around, but Satya, along with Roshan and her other colleagues, began the process of shifting and renovating the space.
She arranged her books, bedding, pieces of art and décor, fabrics, design tools, mannequins, portfolios, appliances, mementos, and every single important or unimportant thing she had brought with her.

As Satya wandered through the house, excited to explore every corner of the place she had longed to call home, her steps halted at the end of the hallway where an old, dusty door stood—a door she hadn't remembered seeing in her childhood visits. It was locked, the wood weathered with age, its brass handle cold to the touch. Despite her efforts to open it, the key was nowhere to be found.

A strange sense of unease settled in, as though this room held memories that no one wanted to uncover—secrets long buried within the walls. For the first time since arriving, excitement gave way to curiosity—and perhaps a little fear—as she realized that this forgotten room might hold the answers to questions she hadn't even thought to ask.

She tugged at the handle, but it didn't budge, the key still nowhere in sight. A chill ran down her spine, a sudden shift from her excitement to something deeper—a growing sense that this room, sealed away for years, hid more than just dust and forgotten furniture.

It felt like a portal to memories long buried, secrets her family had never spoken of, and perhaps truths about her grandfather that she was about to unravel.

And in that moment, she knew—this was only the beginning.

CHAPTER TWO

WHISPERS FROM THE PAST

Satya hadn't realized how unfamiliar a place could feel, even when it was supposed to be home. She stood on the terrace, hoping for a fresh breath of air in the yellow sunlight. Something just didn't feel right. She felt disturbed, and her excitement, like the morning, didn't remain the same. The terrace was open, calm, and fenced in white. She could see the serene landscape and pretty flowers. The sunlight filtered through the bougainvillea leaves. She was sleep-deprived but wanted to find more and settle everything in. Satya had always been a clever and active girl since childhood. The thought of the locked room disturbed her.

As she was cleaning up the shelves, she came across several papers and random notes, which she didn't bother to check or read. As she was dusting her late grandfather's old shelf, a hidden box fell down from the shelf that was tucked and hidden high towards the end. Something inside her told her not to neglect it this time and check it. She curiously yet carefully opened the box. Sudden nervousness struck her soul, and she felt the need to do away with it.

To her surprise, she found random papers, old documents, and diary entries that seemed harmless and absolutely unrelated to her. But what was so special that it was kept in a preserved box like this? She undoubtedly started reading each of them.

As Satya carefully unfolded the letters, she realized that written words hold a different kind of power. They are not just records of the past—they are portals to forgotten emotions, unsaid thoughts, and hidden truths. Written pieces outlast the spoken word; they carry the weight of intention, holding secrets and memories far longer than anyone's voice ever could. The things that a person could never say can only be thoughtfully expressed in a piece of writing.

"Words on paper," Satya thought, "are immortal. They survive through generations, carrying the essence of a person's soul and thoughts long after they're gone."
She opened the first letter, which was half-torn from the sides and sealed with a stamp. It was good enough to read. Satya started:

"Our family was once a strong bond, united by love, trust, and shared values. But times have changed, and I fear that the divisions we've allowed to fester will tear us apart. It was never about money or property, but about pride and decisions made out of fear. What we never spoke about was the day the family split—it wasn't just about disagreements over the inheritance, as everyone was led to believe. There were deeper scars, hidden choices that no one dared to discuss openly.

Decisions were made that changed the course of our family's history, and in time, those decisions drove a wedge between us all. I must confess now, in writing, that I too played a part in this. In fact, a very big role. I believed that silence would protect those I loved, but it only fueled the fire of resentment. I myself destroyed the whole family—the relations, my reputation, trust, everything. I only hope that when this truth is revealed, it is not too late for reconciliation... or redemption. For anyone reading this, I beg you to understand: what you think you know is only the surface of what truly happened. The answers are locked away where no one has looked."

Satya was mature. She sat there for a moment with several thoughts rushing through her mind. A wave of emotions crashed over her: disbelief, confusion, and undeniable curiosity. What her grandfather had written wasn't just about family disagreements—it was about choices that fractured their bond in ways no one ever talked about. Her parents, from her childhood, never explained much to her. They told her stories about how her grandfather was a reputable person in society, for he was a government official. An officer. He was a person with great intellect and humanity. He was a quiet person who kept to himself.
Satya whispered to herself, "There's something I need to know... I want to know."

In her eyes, even though she didn't spend a lot of time with her grandparents, she admired them, and her grandfather was a stoic, reputed figure in the family. She didn't know what they thought about her, but all she knew was that she wanted to spend more time with them. She wanted to understand what it felt like to be in a joint family and to listen to lessons from their forefathers. Her parents raised her with all their will and hard work. She worshipped her parents, and her only aim was to retire them and make them proud. They had lots of expectations from her.

Satya wasn't done yet. She wanted to know every single thing and wanted to unlock the secrets behind the door. She could understand that there was much more to all of this, something no one understood or knew fully. She kept the box carefully with her.

Satya stood in front of the locked door, the weight of her grandfather's words heavy on her heart. The letter had revealed not just family secrets, but also a painful truth: silence and avoidance had only deepened the divisions within their family. She realized then that family wasn't just about shared bloodlines or traditions. It was about confronting the difficult conversations, being vulnerable enough to speak the truths that hurt, and having the courage to bridge the gaps before they became too wide to cross.

In that moment, she understood that to move forward, she needed to unravel the past—not just for herself, but for the legacy of her family. Because without honesty and communication, even the strongest bonds can break. Communication is the ultimate key to building strong and unbreakable relationships.

Satya's eyes lingered on the last lines of the letter again, her pulse quickening. "The answers are locked away where no one has looked." She looked at the sealed door again, realizing it wasn't just a physical barrier—it was symbolic of the family's buried truths. The mention of a deeper rift beyond the inheritance dispute, something about her grandfather's involvement in decisions that tore the family apart, hinted at a secret she wasn't ready to face.

But the scandal... what had he done? And why had he gone to such lengths to hide it? Her fingers traced the edges of the letter, her mind racing. Satya could feel it—this house held more than memories. It held the key to unravelling not just her grandfather's secret, but perhaps the reason the family fell apart.

As she glanced back at the door, she knew that opening it might lead her to answers she wasn't prepared for, but it was the only way forward. She had no choice but to face whatever her grandfather had hidden—because only by doing so could she understand the truth about her family.

CHAPTER THREE

BENEATH THE LEAVES

There were rustling sounds of papers and the creaking of wood coming from the room. This aroused a sense of anxiety within Satya. She eagerly wanted to open the room. As soon as her hand approached the door handle, trying to find a way to open it, there was a knock on the main door. Satya felt disturbed. The atmosphere and her mental state shifted suddenly. She rushed to the main door, thinking it would be Roshan or probably the maid.

To her surprise, it was an old lady, dressed informally, covered with antique jewellery, and with an absolutely wrong choice of colours and silhouettes. It was always the fashion sense and appearances that Satya would notice first in a person—obviously, because that was a part of who she was. Satya was overwhelmed but didn't judge the lady. She seemed to be a nosy, quirky character.

Confused, Satya stood there before the lady broke into conversation.

"I'm Mrs. Roy, your neighbour. I've been living here ever

since this house was built," the old lady introduced herself. Satya invited her in for a cup of tea. Mrs. Roy continued, "Young girl, you wouldn't even understand the beauty and superiority of this ancient family house of yours. Now that you're here after years of dust and wilt, I'm really happy to welcome you to this neighbourhood. I saw you as a kid, but since you only visited during vacations, I didn't get to see you much."

Satya felt comforted by the woman's welcoming attitude.
"I haven't spent much of my time here," Satya replied, "but all that I did brings back a fading sense of nostalgia. I'm really glad that you came by to introduce yourself and greet me."
By then, the cook had brought two rich cups of milk tea and served them. Just then, Roshan called from inside, "Madam, the designs are ready. I would suggest you check them once before packing."
Satya didn't want to leave Mrs. Roy just yet. She was intrigued by the lady's presence and wanted to know more. "Yes, Roshan, I'll be there in 15 minutes," Satya called back, asking him to give them some time.
Mrs. Roy's eyes wandered to the bougainvillea.
"You know, that bougainvillea has been here longer than most of us. It's strange, the way it always seems to grow back, no matter how much you cut it or try to control it. My mother used to say plants like that... they absorb things. Memories, emotions, even secrets. This one especially..." She trailed off, her gaze drifting.

Satya raised an eyebrow, unsure of where the conversation was heading. Mrs. Roy continued, her tone softer but more pointed.

"You ever wonder why it blooms the brightest when no one is around? Almost like it's trying to tell you something. If I were you, I'd pay more attention to the things this house is trying to say, especially what's hiding beneath those leaves."

Satya felt a chill. This was completely unexpected. She had simply wanted to come back to her childhood home and expand her business here. But now, it felt like destiny was leading her down a different path. She felt the importance of knowing everything. Inside, her emotions were a mess.

"What does she mean by hiding beneath those leaves?" Satya thought to herself.

Why had Mrs. Roy suddenly come to her house and started dropping such cryptic hints? Satya felt torn between continuing her investigation and the fear of what she might uncover. There was a growing sense of urgency to learn more about her family.

"Oh, Satya, I'm sorry I wasted your time. You should go and complete your work," Mrs. Roy said, standing up.

"Yeah, sure, aunty. It was really nice meeting you. Please visit often," Satya replied.

Mrs. Roy left, leaving Satya in a confused state. She sat there for a moment, gazing at the bougainvillea. The flowers were beautiful, their vibrant colours covering a large area of the garden. The only sound was the chirping of birds, and the whole atmosphere felt serene. Satya suddenly felt compelled to investigate the flowers more closely.

For some reason, the thought of checking beneath them struck her. She began to dig a little, and soon, she felt something hard. To her surprise, it was a small tin box.

Opening it, she found... a key.

Satya rushed directly toward the locked door without a second thought. As she approached it, her heart raced, and the tension in the air grew thick. She debated whether or not to open the door. What if she uncovered something devastating? The thoughts about her grandfather and family history swirled in her mind.

Finally, she decided to insert the key into the lock. The sound of the key turning echoed through the house. Her hands shook with terror as she unlocked the door. Just as she was about to open it, her phone buzzed loudly, breaking the silence. She jumped slightly, her heart pounding. It was Soha, one of her closest team members from work.

"Hey, Satya, you alright? You've been so off lately," Soha's voice came through, laced with concern.

Satya quickly slipped the key back into her pocket and stepped away from the door, as if someone might see her secret intentions.

"I'm fine," she said, trying to steady her voice. "Just, you know, busy settling things here at my grandparents' place."

Soha paused for a moment. "Yeah, but it's more than that, isn't it? You've been distant. You haven't been yourself since you got there. You're missing meetings, you sound distracted, and I know something's up."

Satya swallowed hard, unsure of how to respond. "It's just the house," she replied weakly. "It's... a lot to take in. Family stuff."

"I get that," Soha said. "I mean, I've had my own share of family drama, but at the end of the day, family is everything, you know? No matter what happens, we're bound by more than just blood. My parents always say that if we don't take care of the ones we love, then what's the point of anything else? We have to find a way to stick together, no matter the difficulties."

Satya's chest tightened. Family. That word felt heavy now, like a reminder of everything she wasn't confronting.

"I appreciate it, Soha," she said quietly. "Really. I'll be okay."

Soha didn't seem fully convinced, but she let it go. "Alright. Just take care of yourself. Don't get lost in that old house, okay?"

As soon as the call ended, Satya stared at the locked door. The very things Soha had said echoed in her mind, only deepening her confusion. Family was the most important thing to her, and she knew there was absolutely nothing wrong with hers. She didn't know much about the extended family, but she knew her parents were the most important people in her life.

Just as she was about to take another step toward the door, her phone rang again. This time, it was her father.

"Satya, beta. How are you? Everything okay at the house?"

Satya froze. There was a tension in her father's voice that she hadn't heard in a long time, as if he knew something but wasn't saying it outright.

"I'm fine, Papa," she said quickly. "Just cleaning up, settling in."

"Good, good. Your mother and I were talking... we're thinking of visiting soon. Maybe this weekend. It's been a long time since we've been back there."

Satya's heart skipped a beat. They're coming? The idea of her parents coming so soon—before she'd uncovered the full truth—made her uneasy. What if they knew more than they were letting on?

"That sounds... great," she said hesitantly. "But you don't need to rush. I'm handling everything fine."

Her father paused. "We'll see. Take care of yourself, beta. Don't get too lost in that old house, okay?"

The same words Soha had used echoed in her father's voice, sending a shiver down Satya's spine. She hung up, her hand trembling slightly as she stared at the door again. The key in her pocket felt heavier now, as if daring her to unlock not just the door, but the secrets buried deep within her family. But something inside her knew—there was more at stake here than just her curiosity.

The closer she got to the truth, the more distant she felt from everything. Knowing the truth would bring significant changes to her life, and with her parents on their way, the pressure to uncover everything before they arrived was almost unbearable. Satya turned away from the door, feeling an unsettling mixture of dread and urgency.

The locked room wasn't just a mystery to solve—it was the key to understanding the fractures within her family. But was she ready for the answers?

As she walked back to the terrace, her eyes caught the bougainvillea leaves once more. They swayed gently in the breeze, casting shadows on the ground. The image felt oddly significant, like they were guarding something deeper, just waiting to be discovered.

CHAPTER FOUR

THREADS OF HERITAGE

In every family, there are invisible threads that bind one generation to the next—threads woven from stories, sacrifices, and the values passed down like heirlooms. These threads remind us that no matter how far we go, our roots always call us back, urging us to honour the past and preserve it for the future. The past must be respected and lessons need to be learned from every single chapter of life that has come our way. Everything and everyone in this world has been put here for a reason. It is all written for us, and there's everything that we deserve.

Satya sat by the window, her eyes tracing the outlines of the house she had only known in fragments of childhood memories. The walls weren't just bricks and cement; they whispered stories of everyone who had come before her. Everyone has a story, but only for those who listen and wish to learn. Her thoughts drifted back to her family. She lived with her father, mother, and brother. She was never much introduced to other family members and she never felt the need to be. She always wished that if her grandparents were there, her life would have been more fulfilling, and she would have loved hearing stories about their life.

Satya knew this wasn't something serious, but why was it being hidden? What was so wrong in telling the truth? She wanted everything exposed because it wasn't just about rediscovering her past; it was about confronting the legacy left behind for her to uncover.

Her phone rang. "Hello? Mama, where are you? I've been waiting..."
"We're on our way, dear. We'll be there in no time."
Satya felt ambivalent. She was happy to see her parents after such a long time, but she still felt stressed. Ten minutes later, her parents arrived. "This place hasn't changed. It's been such a long time since we were last here. This house holds memories," Satya's father exclaimed. Satya came running down the stairs and gave them a hug. "You must be exhausted. Come on in," Satya welcomed them.

They settled into the living room, the air thick with nostalgia. Satya's mother started talking about the past, while her father remained quieter, simply observing. As they sipped tea, the conversation naturally turned to the house and the family's history. "Do you remember how your grandmother used to sit on this very chair? Always with her knitting. She loved talking about everyone in the family and loved exaggerating their habits. You were so little back then," her mother said, smiling at the memories.

Her father sighed, adding, "It's not just the house, Satya.

It's the legacy. Our family has always held certain values—loyalty, tradition, and respect. These aren't just words; they're what kept us together through everything." Satya's father was a man of great values. He was quiet, just like his father, and always followed in his father's footsteps. He missed his father deeply but rarely expressed it in front of others.

Later, Satya's father took her aside for a more serious conversation in the garden. "I know you've been asking questions about the house, Satya. About the family. But some things... some things are better left alone."

"You're always so vague, Papa. I know you're hiding something, and I know there's something here," Satya pushed, her frustration building.

Her father sighed again, trying to convince her to focus on her work and future. "You have a brighter future, Satya. I don't want you to waste time on these things. The truth, sometimes, is painful. This house... it holds more than just memories. It holds burdens. And I don't want you to carry them."

As her father walked away, Satya was left alone in the garden. Her mind wandered back to her childhood, recalling small but vivid memories: her grandmother cooking in the kitchen, her grandfather reading, and her father's quiet presence. At dinner, the conversation shifted to family values. Her mother, speaking in a calm, motherly tone, imparted wisdom as if delivering lifelong lessons. "You know, Satya, family isn't just about blood. It's about love, commitment, and sometimes, sacrifice. We've all had to make hard choices for the sake of this family. And I know your father has his own burdens to bear."

Satya continued to search for the truth. "I don't want you to think I'm keeping things from you out of cruelty. I just want you to understand that some things are best left in the past. The house... it's part of our family, but it doesn't define who you are." Satya listened quietly, feeling the weight of her parents' words but still drawn to the mystery of the locked room.

That night was difficult for her. She couldn't sleep well. The next morning, her parents had to leave for their respective routines and jobs. "Dear, please remember what your papa and I have told you," her mother said as they prepared to leave, hoping Satya would take their advice to heart. "We're always with you, and we're proud of you," her father added, bringing a sense of hope to her.

Satya felt pleased with their words. She was happy that they were proud of her, and their satisfaction was her greatest motivation. But this was just the beginning. As Satya continued her search for answers without opening the door, she stumbled upon an old book. Inside, she found a piece of paper. Assuming it was just like any other, she almost threw it away. But the wind outside blew the paper back onto her table. It was old, yellowed, and folded between the pages of the book. She took it as a sign and opened it.

"To my trusted friend,
The time has come to make our move. We've waited long enough, and the weight of our cause grows heavier each day.

The children must not know—not yet. If we fail, they will be protected. But if we succeed, they will understand why we made these sacrifices. You know where to find me when the time is right. We cannot afford to be careless now, not with so much at stake. Trust only those whose loyalty is proven. The truth will not remain buried forever.
—D."

Satya didn't feel nervous or confused. Instead, she felt a surge of determination, knowing she was closer to the truth than ever before. Her grandfather had been working for a cause, something important, and Satya had been right all along. She knew her grandfather could never be wrong. It was now up to her to restore the legacy and uncover the hidden truth

CHAPTER FIVE

SECRETS UNLOCKED

Satya sat on the edge of her bed, staring at the worn piece of paper she had found that day. The words on it had consumed her thoughts, leaving her restless, caught between wanting to move forward and fearing what she might uncover next. "The truth will not remain buried forever." The line echoed in her mind like a warning and a promise. What was the truth? And why was it hidden in the first place?

For the first time in her life, she felt the weight of her family's history pressing down on her, urging her to uncover what had been lost. She glanced at the clock. The house was quiet. Her parents had left, and there was no one to stop her now. Taking a deep breath, she stood up, grabbed the keys, and made her way toward the door that had been locked for as long as she could remember. She unlocked it, this time without hesitation.

As soon as she opened the door, it felt like any other dusty room. It seemed like it was sealed since ages. The atmosphere was heavy with a mix of silence and musty air. Faint light crept from the hallway, illuminating the dust particles dancing in the air. The room felt cold and distant, the kind of place that had been untouched by time but still carried the weight of memories. The old wood creaked as she walked in.

She was astonished by the essence of the room, and every object in the room spoke to her. Every small sound echoed louder than it should and made the moment more surreal. It felt like Satya could hear her heartbeat.

The thick, old air seemed to carry whispers from the past, almost as if the room itself was alive, guarding the secrets it held. She found an ink pen that had her grandfather's name carved on it. Then she came across a chair that had various Indian patterns carved on it. Everything was beautifully detailed.

Just as Satya moved forward trying to find more significant pieces, she came across a journal. Out of curiosity, she opened it to read. Initially, when Satya started discovering, she was confused and afraid. But now that she was finding clues and was getting closer to knowing the truth, she felt amazed by every single thing she came across. She was no longer terrified or hesitant.

Inside the journal, Satya discovered handwritten entries in her grandfather's familiar, neat script. As she flipped through the pages, the entries revealed not just personal reflections but detailed accounts of a hidden struggle—a cause that he had devoted himself to but had kept secret from the family. The journal was not a diary of everyday events but a meticulous record of plans and alliances.

She was casually flipping the pages and reading random accounts of his daily life. But one such writing caught her eye.

"The decision is final. Our goal is not to create chaos but to restore balance where it has long been absent. For too many years, the people of our town have been manipulated by those in power. Their voices have been silenced, and their struggles overlooked. The small farmers, the workers—they all deserve justice. The system needs to change, and it begins with us. Our efforts will not be violent, but they will be relentless. We will fight with truth, with determination, and with unity."

Satya had a clear picture in her mind. She felt empowered and extremely happy seeing that her grandfather was doing nothing wrong but working for such an important cause. She always stood for justice.

Another entry read:

"The leaders have agreed. The movement must stay underground for now. We cannot risk exposure—not yet. Too many lives depend on our success. I've seen the impact of corruption, and I cannot stand by while it continues to harm those who trust us. The plan is in motion, but we must tread carefully. Our allies are in place, and the strategy is sound. But we cannot let our families bear the consequences of failure. If something happens to me, this journal must remain hidden. Only when the time is right should these truths come to light."

Satya turned the page and found another entry:

"We're close. The network is growing, and more are joining our cause each day. I have kept this from the family not out

of shame, but out of protection. The less they know, the safer they are. But if the day comes when they find this journal, I want them to know that everything I did was for them—for our future. The risks we take today are to ensure they never have to face the same hardships we endured. Truth will always prevail."

Even though her grandfather wasn't a victim of all this, he wanted to stand up for those who were silenced. He was a quiet person, but his mind and ideas spoke louder.

As Satya read further, the entries outlined key meetings with local leaders and activists, plans to expose corrupt officials, and a vision for a more just society. It became clear that her grandfather had been leading a movement to challenge the local government's control over land and resources, aiming to return power to the people. This was the "cause" he had been working on in secret, a cause that could have placed the family in danger if revealed at the time.

The final entry struck Satya the hardest:

"This will be my last entry for now. The movement is on the brink of success, but I fear it has attracted too much attention. The authorities are watching, and our allies are becoming targets. I cannot risk bringing this danger home. If anything happens to me, let this journal serve as a testament to what we fought for. Justice, equality, and a future where every voice matters. My children, if any of you are reading this—know that the path I walked was not easy, but it was necessary. And now, it is your turn to decide how you will carry forward our legacy."

Satya closed the journal, her heart racing. She realized her grandfather had sacrificed so much for the greater good, and now, she had to decide what to do with the knowledge she had uncovered. There was an inner conflict going on inside her. There was pride, joy, confusion, and also fear that if anyone else found out about her discovery, it would put her in trouble. How would she face her father, who asked her not to dig into all this? She was in a confused state, thinking about the consequences and whether to keep digging further or not. She wanted to know the reason for the family breaking up over a dispute. But she didn't want her father to be disappointed.

Satya now had access to everything. She kept everything aside and went to her office to check on some new designs. When life becomes so chaotic and you feel like you're not able to balance anything, your work or hobby acts as an escape. Doing what you love and feel positive in is worth leaving everything at that time. Mental peace is extremely valuable.

Satya was smart enough and mature too, but all of this wasn't her choice. It was something that was meant to happen, so it did. Nothing was wrong about it, but the thoughts struck her head every time. Roshan, who had been observant, tried asking her if she was fine or overthinking about something, but Satya always denied it. Roshan decided to inform her parents about the same. He thought that Satya was feeling overwhelmed after coming to such a huge, old place after years of working abroad. He called her dad about the same.

Father knew what all of this was about and decided to confront her. Her phone rang.

"Hi Papa, I'm actually in my office working on some patterns. Could you please call after some time?"

"Satya, it's urgent. You too, spare me some of your time, and you can do your work later." He sounded disappointed. Satya panicked. "Sure then, if it's urgent, I'm here to hear you."

"I told you to stay away from all of that. Beta, why don't you understand that it was all in the past and it had nothing to do with you! Why don't you just keep all of these unnecessary things aside and focus on what you're actually here for? What's so interesting and important about knowing all of this?"

Satya was embarrassed and unhappy with whatever her father had said.

"Hmm... I understand. I'm not doing any of that. I'll call you later. Please don't mind."

Satya hung up. It felt like a huge burden on her now. "Maybe I should actually focus on my work and leave this. I've known enough," Satya thought to herself and went to her room to take some rest.

CHAPTER SIX

UNSEEN FORCES

Satya sat at her desk, her head resting in her hands. She had told herself she would focus on her work, bury herself in patterns, colours, and designs, but her thoughts kept drifting back to the journal. The more she tried to forget about all of it, the more she thought about it. The revelations she had uncovered were more than just family secrets; they were fragments of a history that had shaped her without her knowing. She wasn't just discovering her grandfather's past—she was rediscovering her own identity.

The sound of the rain tapping against the windows filled the room. It was a quiet, almost soothing noise, but it did nothing to calm the storm inside Satya's mind. She thought about her father's words during their last call. His voice had been stern, almost desperate, as he urged her to leave everything alone. But how could she? The truth was so close, and she had already uncovered too much to simply walk away. She was the one who started all of this, and certainly she had to end it all too. Either on a bitter note or doing something for it.

The journal still lay on her desk, as if calling to her. Satya picked it up again, her fingers tracing the worn leather cover. She remembered the last entry she had read—her grandfather's final words before he went silent. There were still unanswered questions, still pieces of the puzzle missing. And now that she had begun, she couldn't stop.

Just as Satya was about to open the journal again, there was a knock at the door. She frowned. No one was supposed to come to the office this late, especially not with the weather being so bad.

"Come in," she called out, expecting one of her colleagues to appear with a work-related issue.

The door opened slowly, and to her surprise, it wasn't someone from work. Instead, it was an elderly man, hunched over with age, holding a worn umbrella in one hand and a large, old-fashioned bag in the other. His face was weathered, his clothes simple but neat, and his eyes, though clouded with age, held a sharpness that unnerved her.

"Uhm... hello sir. I certainly don't recognise you. How can I help you?" Satya asked, standing up from her desk.

"You don't know me," he finally said, his voice gravelly and deep. "But I knew your grandfather."

Satya's heart skipped a beat. The air in the room seemed to change, thickening with tension as the man's words hung in the space between them. How could he know about her grandfather? No one else had spoken of him since she had started uncovering his past.

"I... I'm sorry, but who are you?" Satya stammered, her

mind racing to catch up.

The man sat on a chair wiping his face with a handkerchief. "You don't need to know who I am," he said with a serious tone. "I know what you're up to these days. Just remember it's dangerous. You need to be cautious."

Satya got chills. Who was he? How did he know all this? Was he keeping an eye on her? She felt like she was being watched by everyone. She tried not to lose her calm.

"I don't know what you're talking about," she said, trying to maintain her composure. "I think you have the wrong person."

The man shook his head slowly. "No. I don't. I was part of it—back when your grandfather was still alive. We worked together, him and me, on the same cause. And now that you've started looking into it, there are others who are paying attention."

Satya's mouth went dry. Others? Who others? Now what's this new fuss about? She tried keeping all these things to herself and tried being secretive. Her grandfather's warnings echoed in her mind. The movement must stay underground for now... Too many lives depend on our success.

Satya could barely believe what she was hearing. She hadn't considered that her search for answers might put her in real danger, that her curiosity could have such far-reaching consequences.

"What do you mean?" Satya asked, her voice barely a whisper.

"I mean that your grandfather wasn't just fighting a few corrupt officials. He was taking on something much bigger than corrupt officials. A network—deeply rooted in politics and business—people who'd stop at nothing to protect their interests. Even now, their reach is powerful. They've made sure no one digs too deep, especially into what your grandfather uncovered."

Satya's chest tightened. She had expected some resistance from her family, maybe some reluctance to confront the past, but this? This was something else entirely. This was a threat.

"Why are you telling me this?" she asked. "If it's so dangerous, why come to me now?"

The man leaned back in his chair, his gaze softening just slightly.

"Because your grandfather was a good man. He believed in justice, in doing the right thing, no matter the cost. I owe it to him to make sure his legacy isn't forgotten. But you have to be careful. He never wanted his family to get into trouble or be a part of any of this. There are forces at work here that you don't fully understand."

She never imagined that this thing would cause such a big mess. She thought that everything in this house revolved around her and no one knew about anything.

"What should I do?" she asked, her voice trembling.

The man stood up, grabbing his umbrella once more. "That's for you to decide," he said quietly. "But remember this—there's more at stake here than just your family's history. Be smart, Satya. Don't let curiosity lead you into something you can't get out of."

Without another word, the man turned and left the office, leaving Satya standing there, her mind reeling from the encounter. She wanted to chase after him, to demand more answers, but something held her back. Maybe it was fear. Maybe it was the realization that she was now part of something far bigger than herself.

She sat back down, her eyes drifting once again to the journal. The answers she sought were right there, within reach. But now, for the first time, she hesitated. How much was she willing to risk for the truth?

As the door closed behind the mysterious man, Satya's mind whirled. Why now? She had barely scratched the surface of her grandfather's work, yet the sense of danger was already looming large. If what the man said was true—that her grandfather had been fighting against a powerful system—why had no one come after her family before? Why, after all these years, was her investigation suddenly triggering such a strong reaction?

She picked up the journal again, staring at the cryptic notes scrawled across the yellowed pages. The thought gnawed at her. It didn't make sense. Her grandfather had gone since years, and whatever secret movement he had been part of had long since faded into obscurity. Had something changed? Or had the passage of time simply made those secrets even more dangerous?

Satya's phone buzzed on the desk, breaking her thoughts. She grabbed it and saw a message from her cousin, Raj.
"Satya, I'm not one to meddle in family affairs, but I think you should stop whatever you're doing. Something about Grandpa's past—just... be careful. There are things happening that I never wanted to get involved in, but now we all might be."

Satya was shocked. Raj was one of the most distant person who had no interest in any of the family affairs. He never attended any functions and also never thought of keeping contact with any cousins. For him to reach out to Satya that too with such a cryptic message was unusual. She typed back quickly:

"What do you mean? How do you know?"
The reply came almost instantly: "I've been hearing things. There are people connected to that time who are still around. Some of them are in positions of power now. They're nervous. Grandpa's work didn't just die with him."

Satya's hands trembled as she stared at the screen. Pieces of the puzzle began to shift into place. The movement her grandfather had been part of—whatever it had been—hadn't just been about corruption in their small town or a few officials. It had touched on something larger, something that had reached into the present day. The system still exists, she realized. And it's watching.

But why now? She shot off another message: "Why is this becoming a problem after so long?"
Raj's response was brief, but it carried weight: "Because people with power never forget. And they've kept an eye on us all this time. Your digging is reopening old wounds. They see it as a threat."

Satya sat back in her chair, her mind racing. She hadn't realized how deep this went, or that her actions would ripple so far. But now she understood—her investigation wasn't just about the past. It was about the present. The secrets her grandfather had tried to expose all those years ago still had relevance today, and there were powerful people who would do anything to keep them buried.

Now what was next? Satya had to choose.

Satya felt the weight of her decision settling in. She could walk away, pretend none of this ever mattered, like her father had asked her to. But the journal lay before her, full of answers that had been buried for too long. If she moved forward, she'd be stepping into the unknown—where danger lurked. Yet, something in her knew she couldn't simply turn back now. She had to choose: face the truth, no matter the cost, or walk away, leaving everything unresolved.

CHAPTER SEVEN

DOORSTEP LETTER

The rain had finally slowed to a gentle drizzle after hours of relentless downpour. Satya sat at her desk, staring at the worn journal in front of her, unable to shake the unease that had been building all evening. The storm outside seemed to mirror the chaos in her mind, but as the rain tapered off, so did her thoughts. She needed to clear her head, and the fresh air outside, with the city still shimmering in the aftermath of the rain, seemed like the perfect escape.

She grabbed her coat and made her way out of the building. Whenever Satya was tense and couldn't think of anything, she felt a walk would do the best for her. So, she decided to step out of the house for a bit and come back with an idea. The air was cool, carrying the scent of damp earth and wet pavement. Her footsteps echoed softly as she walked aimlessly, letting the rhythm of her steps calm her racing thoughts. The streets were quiet now, only the occasional car passing by, splashing through puddles.

Just as she was approaching the main gate, she stepped on a letter. Again, a letter. She was sick of finding letters by now. But this time, it wasn't her who searched for it, but it was there to give her a message. Her heart was racing, anticipating what could be inside.

The letter was simple and neat, with no signature. It read:

"Step back before it hits you hard. You have nothing to do with all this. Save yourself and don't drag yourself and your family into this. This has been continuing, and it will. It's completely harmless for you unless you provoke it once more. You are in danger, so is Raj."

The message was short but straight. Satya felt petrified. Who could have sent this? Why wasn't there any signature? Is she being watched 24/7? How does this person know about the investigation? Such thoughts haunted her. She glanced around, but the street was empty. With no one in sight, she tucked the envelope into her coat pocket and hurried back inside.

She knew, somehow, that this was connected to the man who had come to her weeks ago with vague warnings about her grandfather's past. Her mind raced as she re-read the words. Raj—her cousin, her closest confidante—was being watched. By whom? And why? She felt disturbed because he was also being dragged into all this because of her.

Just then, a flash of movement outside her window caught her attention. Satya's heart skipped a beat as she peered out into the dark. A shadowy figure stood at the corner of the street, barely visible in the dim streetlight, but watching her apartment intently. Her pulse quickened. Raj was being followed, and now, it seemed, so was she.

Satya immediately drew the curtains. She was unable to process anything. Her phone buzzed on the table, breaking the silence. It was Raj.

"Satya, I–something's wrong," Raj stuttered on the other end. He wasn't as confident as usual. "I'm being followed.

Someone's been following me for a while. It doesn't feel right."

Satya's stomach lurched. "Raj, don't worry, keep driving, okay? Head to the old warehouse by the docks. I'll meet you there. And be careful—they're watching both of us." She tried to keep her voice steady, even though she was scared to death.

Satya hung up, her mind already running through what little information she had. Her grandfather had left behind a legacy—a fight against corruption that had cost him his life. But now, the very people he had fought against seemed to have resurfaced. They had found Raj, and now they were after her, too.

She couldn't waste any more time. Throwing on her jacket and grabbing her car keys, Satya slipped the letter into her bag. Her thoughts raced as she headed for the door, her footsteps quick and quiet. As she stepped outside, she cautiously glanced down the street. The shadowy figure was gone, but that didn't make her feel any safer. Whoever they were, they wouldn't disappear so easily.

She hurried towards the warehouse by the docks—a place her grandfather had used to hide his papers, to plan his moves against the very men who now sought to silence his family. The cold night air bit at her face as she arrived at the docks, the warehouse looming large in front of her. She spotted Raj's car parked near the entrance, and a wave of relief washed over her.

But as she got closer, she noticed something off—Raj's car door was slightly ajar. As she rushed forward, her hand reaching for the door handle, she saw Raj slumped against the steering wheel, unconscious but breathing. His phone lay on the seat beside him, the screen still on.

She was just about to try waking him up when two figures approached her in the pitch dark. Their movements were slow. Satya's breath caught as the two figures came into view. One of them stepped forward, and the dim streetlight illuminated his face—it was the same man who had left the letter at her doorstep. His expression was hard to read, a mix of tension and something else, something that made her unsure of his intentions. The other man remained in the shadows, silent.

The old man who had been in her office earlier came closer to her and spoke in a low voice.

"You should've read the letter more carefully," the man said, his voice low but steady. "I warned you. This isn't about just you anymore."

Satya narrowed her eyes, her hand tightening around her bag. "What do you want from us? Why are you following Raj? I thought you were with my grandfather," she said, feeling deceived.

Satya's mind raced. The man had once fought against the corrupt powers her grandfather had stood up to, but now...was he trying to help her or trap her? The weight of the letter pressed against her mind, the words suddenly more urgent than ever.

"You were once against them," she said, trying to piece it together. "Now you're working with them?"

The man's jaw clenched. "I don't work with anyone anymore. But I know how they operate. And right now, they're closer than you think."

A flicker of movement caught her eye—behind him, in the distance, a car pulled up, its headlights cutting through the rain. Satya's pulse quickened.

"Get Raj out of here," the man said, his voice sharp now. "And don't come back to this place. They're using it to track you.”

Before Satya could ask more, the man turned and walked away, his silhouette blending into the rainy night, leaving her with more questions than answers.

CHAPTER EIGHT

CONTINUING THE LEGACY

Satya couldn't stop thinking about the man's words as she drove back home. She felt betrayed and never expected someone to switch sides after fighting for justice. Rain soaked the streets and Raj was still unconscious. Her thoughts raced, replaying the events of the last few hours. The letter, the man's cryptic warning, the dark figures following them—it all pointed to something bigger than she'd anticipated. Her grandfather's legacy had put her and Raj in the crosshairs of dangerous people. She had to figure out how to finish what he started, no matter the cost.

The weather was bad, constantly raining. It had picked up again by the time they reached their house. Satya managed to get Raj inside, laying him gently on the couch. As she waited for him to wake up, she paced back and forth, her mind swirling with possibilities. The old man—her grandfather's ally, once a fierce opponent of corruption—was now entangled with the very people he had fought. But why? And how was she supposed to stop them when she didn't even know who "they" were?

She wanted to put an end to this already. Sometimes she was proud that she was able to continue her grandfather's legacy but the other times she felt as if all this was pointless. They were never the victims of the whole thing so why were they fighting for justice? But humanity lies in understanding the depth and pain of other beings. If one cannot connect and help another person in pain; no one can certainly help them in need. Justice is a right given to every individual. Everyone deserves to be treated fairly and live their life without being compelled to anything.

Raj stirred, groaning softly as he came to. His eyes fluttered open, and he looked around, disoriented.

"What...what happened?" he asked, his voice hoarse.

"You were followed," Satya said, sitting down beside him. "We both were. Someone left me a letter—warning us to stay out of this. But Raj, I can't. Grandfather's work, his fight—it's not over. And I think they're trying to bury it for good."

Raj sat up straighter, the tension clear in his face. "So what do we do now?"

Satya stood, her resolve hardening. "We won't back down. I'll finish what he started."

She crossed the room, pulling out an old, leather-bound book from her bag. It had been her grandfather's journal—filled with notes, plans, and everything he had gathered during his years of fighting corruption. She placed it on the table in front of Raj.

"I've been going through his notes," she said, flipping through the pages. "There's a pattern. He had started uncovering something big, something that involved high-ranking officials. I think that's why they went after him. But he never finished—he left behind clues, pieces of information, but no conclusion. If we can figure out what he knew, we might be able to expose them."

Raj frowned, leaning closer to the journal. "But if they're watching us, won't it be dangerous to keep digging?"

"It will," Satya admitted. "But we don't have a choice. If we don't continue this, they'll keep coming after us—and worse, they'll get away with it."

Raj nodded, determination replacing the fear in his eyes. "Alright, let's do it. But we need to be smart. We can't just walk into their trap."

Satya agreed. She spent the rest of the night going through her grandfather's notes, trying to piece together the connections he had made. Every page seemed to hold another clue, another thread to follow. Raj, still recovering, helped as best as he could, offering insight into some of the people and places mentioned in the journal.

By morning, they had a plan. Satya would continue her grandfather's work, quietly investigating the corruption that had taken root. She would be cautious, keeping a low profile while gathering evidence. Raj would help, but from a distance—keeping an eye on anyone who might be watching them and making sure they stayed one step ahead.

As they prepared to leave the apartment, Satya felt a sense of purpose she hadn't felt before. Her grandfather had fought for justice, and now it was her turn to carry on his legacy. She wasn't just going to sit back and let the corrupt win—she was going to finish what he started, no matter the cost.

Raj was bringing pieces together, "You know, Satya, it's strange... how all of this started because of family. Grandfather—he did everything he could to protect us, to make sure we lived in a better world. And here we are, years later, still fighting that battle."

Satya paused, looking at Raj thoughtfully. "I've been thinking the same thing. This fight—it's not just about the corruption or the injustice. It's about what Grandfather stood for. Family is about more than just blood—it's about standing up for what's right, even when it's not easy."

Raj nodded slowly. "We could have walked away, left it all behind. But family... we owe it to him, to ourselves, to finish what he started. He taught us that justice is worth fighting for, even when it feels impossible."

Satya smiled faintly. "He also taught us that we're stronger together. No matter how dark things get, we have each other's backs. And that's why we'll win this—we won't let them take away what Grandfather built."

Raj smiled back, the weight of the situation still heavy but somehow easier to bear. "You're right. We'll figure this out—together."

Satya stood, reaching for her coat. "Let's go. We've got work to do, and I have a feeling Grandfather left us more than just clues in that journal. He always believed in doing the right thing, and so do we."

As they stepped out into the morning light, the storm finally behind them, Satya felt a renewed sense of purpose. This wasn't just her fight—it was their family's fight. It was about legacy, justice, and making sure the world they lived in was a little bit better, one step at a time.

CHAPTER NINE

UNVEILING THE TRUTH

Satya's fingers ran over the boxes and stacks of papers her grandfather had left behind. Somewhere in this mess was the key to unravelling the web of corruption that had cost him his life. Raj, still pale from their recent ordeal, was beside her, sifting through piles of documents with equal determination.

"This has to be it," Satya muttered, her voice echoing slightly in the vast, empty space. "Grandfather wouldn't have left us without answers."

After hours of searching, her hand brushed against something unusual. Hidden beneath old ledgers was a small, weathered envelope, yellowed with age but carefully sealed. It wasn't addressed to her—or to anyone she knew. Curious, she opened the letter, her heart racing. The contents were cryptic at first glance but contained names and locations that sent a chill down her spine.

This letter wasn't meant for her—it was a communication

between two people deeply involved in the very corruption her grandfather had tried to expose.

"Raj, look at this," she said, handing him the paper. His eyes scanned the lines, widening as he realized the importance of what they had found.

"This... this is it. This is the proof we've been missing." The letter pointed towards a larger corruption scheme involving shady land deals and misuse of public funds. It read:

To our trusted partner,
The recent transaction involving the development contracts has been successfully processed. Ensure that the records reflect the revised values we discussed, and make sure the land title transfer remains hidden until we finalize the next phase. Any outside attention must be diverted. Leverage your position to make sure there are no investigations or inquiries into our recent activities. We cannot afford any disruptions. The funds from the special project should be routed as planned. Keep this within our inner circle and confirm that the local authorities remain uninvolved. Expect further instructions when the final approval comes through.
Regards,
V.K.

Probably, this was something the man had left at the warehouse, or perhaps her grandfather had stumbled upon it and kept it safe with the intention of confronting V.K. or protecting the evidence. Over time, the letter had been overlooked amidst other papers, but its presence now provided crucial evidence linking V.K. and others to the corruption. Now Satya could piece together the extent of the fraud, showing how deeply embedded it was and how many layers of deceit were involved in the scandal.

As the hours passed, everything started falling into place, making more sense. The letter now represented a smoking gun—direct proof of the illicit dealings that her grandfather might have been aware of but couldn't expose during his lifetime. Satya had nothing to lose now. She was confident and smart enough to handle this, and nothing could stop her now that she was so close. The chapter was finally taking a turn.
Raj, who had once distanced himself from family matters, was now fully invested in protecting their grandfather's legacy. Life had a way of pulling people into the most unexpected battles.

Along with the letter, Satya found several more pieces of evidence that helped them lay the foundation for their plan. She discovered a photograph involving other people still alive to this day. They were known government officials, making it easier for her to track them down and extract more information. She also uncovered old financial records indicating money transfers to offshore accounts, all linked to shell companies controlled by corrupt officials. This confirmed the embezzlement and illegal wealth accumulation that had cost countless lives and livelihoods.

Invoices and tax filings from these companies showed significant discrepancies, proving that her grandfather had been on the brink of exposing a massive tax fraud scheme. The betrayal ran deep: government officials had acquired land from farmers and working-class communities under the guise of public development projects—promising compensation that never materialized or was far below the land's value. The officials then sold or leased the land to private companies, leaving the farmers displaced with no land or livelihood.

This was the very injustice her grandfather had fought against. Public funds were mismanaged, and essential public works were left unfinished or in disrepair, further impoverishing those who needed help the most.

Satya and Raj had a clear picture in their minds now. They realized that they couldn't fight this battle alone. Together, they began reaching out to others who had once been loyal to her grandfather or had been affected by the corruption. They approached Roshan, Soha, Mrs. Roy, and many others who were ready to help.

These allies provided additional information, giving them the strength and resources to move forward. Together, they gathered more concrete evidence—bank records, land contracts, and testimonies from affected individuals. With their teamwork and determination, they were closer to achieving their goal than ever.

Yet, even as things seemed to be progressing smoothly, Satya felt the weight of responsibility pressing on her. The evidence they had uncovered was dangerous and could put them all at risk.

"Satya, please be cautious. I hope you don't get hurt. This is our fight, and we'll fight it together—not just for Grandfather but for every single life that's been affected," Raj said, trying to lift her spirits.

"You're right. We'll fight this and see it through to the end. With you guys by my side, I feel like I can achieve anything," Satya said with renewed hope.

Satya and Raj had long suspected they were being watched, but it wasn't until they found the old documents among her grandfather's belongings that their suspicions were confirmed. As they sifted through the papers, a particular file caught Raj's eye.

Upon closer inspection, they realized the documents were surveillance reports—detailed logs of whom her grandfather had been in contact with, where he had traveled, and what meetings he had attended. Someone had been monitoring her grandfather's every move for years. But it wasn't just him—they were being watched too.

Raj found another report that detailed their movements. It described how Raj had been seen speaking with Satya near the warehouse where they'd first uncovered her grandfather's evidence. Every meeting, every journey had been noted.

"This is why we've been one step behind," Satya said, her voice tense. "They knew exactly where we were going and what we were looking for."

The final confirmation came when Satya found an old, discarded bugging device tucked away in the corner of the warehouse. It was small and easily overlooked, but the moment she recognized it, the truth became clear: they had been listening in all along.

"They've been watching us the whole time," Raj added grimly. "But now we have proof."
This discovery shifted everything. Their enemies weren't just hiding evidence—they were actively preventing them from uncovering it. Satya's mind raced as the weight of their situation sunk in. Knowing they were being watched made every move more dangerous, but it also gave them a sense of urgency. They couldn't afford to slow down now.

"We need to use this against them," Satya said, her voice filled with determination. "They've been watching us, but we can turn the tables. If we go public with this, they'll have no place to hide."

Raj nodded, already planning their next steps. "But we have to be smart. We can't let them know we've figured it out. We need to act like everything's normal while we prepare to expose them."

With the surveillance reports, hidden documents, and the bugging device as concrete evidence, they were closer than ever to blowing the lid off the corruption that had plagued her grandfather's life and the people he fought for. But they still needed more. They needed the final pieces to tie the corrupt officials directly to the suffering of farmers, workers, and everyday people.

As they delved deeper into the files, they found reports detailing unethical land deals—agreements that had robbed local farmers of their land and livelihoods. Her grandfather had been trying to block these deals, but after his death, they had gone through without opposition. The farmers were displaced, forced into poverty, while the land was used for industrial projects benefiting only the rich and powerful.

"This is it," Satya said, holding up the documents. "This is how they did it. They destroyed everything my grandfather stood for. We have to make sure people know the truth."

Raj glanced at her, the weight of their mission clear in his eyes. "It's time to take this public."

With evidence in hand and a plan forming, Satya and Raj prepared for the final confrontation. They would reveal everything, bring justice to those who had suffered, and finally honour her grandfather's legacy. The road ahead was dangerous, but Satya was no longer afraid. She had a purpose, and she wouldn't stop until the truth was known.

This was their turning point. The fight was just beginning.

CHAPTER TEN

THE FINAL CONFRONTATION

The air was thick with anticipation. Satya stood before the mirror, her hands slightly trembling as she adjusted the microphone on her lapel. The press conference was just minutes away, and her heart raced at the thought of what was about to unfold.

She caught a glimpse of Raj, pacing back and forth, his face reflecting the same mixture of determination and anxiety that coursed through her veins.

"You ready for this?" Raj asked, his voice steady despite the tension in the room.

Satya nodded, her mind running over the mountain of evidence they had gathered. The stolen lands, the offshore accounts, the surveillance reports—it all led to this moment.

"There's no going back now," she replied, taking a deep breath. "Everything depends on what we do next."

Outside the small room, the noise of reporters and cameras

setting up was growing louder. They had managed to get a major news outlet to cover the event, ensuring that the truth would be broadcast across the country. But with that came risk. The people they were about to expose were powerful, and Satya knew they wouldn't go down without a fight.

"Do you think they'll try to stop us?" she asked, her voice lowering to a whisper.

Raj stopped pacing and looked at her with a calm, reassuring gaze. "They've already tried everything. Intimidation, surveillance, bribes. But we're still here, aren't we? They're the ones who should be worried now."

A knock on the door interrupted them. It was Soha, her face serious but calm. "We're ready for you," she said. "It's time." Satya exhaled slowly, pushing down the last remnants of doubt.

She had spent her whole life running from this fight, from the shadow her grandfather's legacy cast over her. But now, standing on the brink of the biggest moment in her life, she felt a sense of peace. This was where she was meant to be. Together with Raj, she walked toward the stage, the weight of the moment pressing down on her.

The curtains parted, revealing a sea of reporters, cameras flashing, and microphones pointed in their direction. Satya stepped up to the podium, her hands gripping the edges tightly. The room fell silent, all eyes on her. This was it. The moment the truth would finally come to light.

Satya cleared her throat, the weight of her grandfather's

legacy pressing on her. The words she had prepared danced in her mind, but the emotions of the moment made it difficult to find her voice. The room was silent, save for the occasional click of a camera.

All eyes were on her—waiting, watching. "Good afternoon," she began, her voice firm but quiet. "We are here today to reveal the truth. The truth that has been hidden for too long, buried under layers of corruption, deceit, and betrayal."

The reporters leaned in, sensing the gravity of what was about to come. Raj stood beside her, scanning the crowd, ready to support her if she faltered. But Satya didn't waver. She was done running from the truth.

"For years, my grandfather fought to expose the injustices that were being committed against the common people of this country—farmers, workers, everyday citizens who trusted their leaders to protect their rights," she continued. "But instead, those in power took advantage of that trust. They stole from the people, using their authority to fill their own pockets, while others suffered." She paused, letting the weight of her words sink in. The room remained silent, tense with expectation. "What we are about to show you will not only prove the extent of this corruption, but it will also reveal the individuals responsible. These are not just minor acts of greed. These are crimes that have devastated lives, destroyed livelihoods, and left entire communities in ruins."

Raj stepped forward, pulling out a folder filled with documents—evidence they had spent weeks collecting. He handed the first few pages to the nearest reporters. Satya continued as the papers were passed around.

"We have uncovered evidence of illegal land deals, fraudulent financial schemes, and the use of public funds for private gain. The very people who were meant to serve and protect the citizens of this country have been complicit in these crimes."

The tension in the room grew thicker as reporters read through the documents, their expressions shifting from curiosity to shock. Satya knew this was just the beginning. What came next would change everything.

Raj handed over the final document, a piece of undeniable proof that tied together all the scattered pieces of corruption they had been investigating. Satya looked at the crowd of reporters, many of them already scribbling furiously in their notepads, preparing to break the story.

The cameras zoomed in on her, capturing her every word, every breath. "I want to make one thing clear," she said, her voice firm. "This isn't just about my family. My grandfather wasn't the only one affected by this. Thousands of innocent people were. The farmers who lost their land, the workers who were cheated of their wages, the families who were forced into poverty—all of them are the victims of this greed. And it's time that the people responsible for their suffering are held accountable."

The room erupted in murmurs as the weight of what she was saying hit the audience. Reporters leaned forward, asking questions all at once, trying to get more details, but

Satya raised a hand, silencing them. "We have provided the evidence," she said. "Now it's up to the authorities to act. It's up to all of us to ensure that justice is served." Raj glanced at her, his eyes filled with admiration. He had seen her struggle with this, seen how hard it had been to go through the evidence, to confront the truth about her grandfather's life and death. But now, she stood strong, her conviction clear.

The press conference ended, and as the reporters filed out, Raj turned to Satya. "You were incredible," he said softly. "I don't think they were expecting that." Satya smiled weakly, the adrenaline finally wearing off. "I just hope it's enough," she said. "This is just the beginning. We've brought the truth to light, but now we have to make sure that something is actually done about it." Raj nodded. "And we will. Together."

As they walked out of the press room, Satya felt a sense of relief wash over her. It wasn't over yet, but they had taken the first step. They had finally brought the truth into the light. As Satya and Raj stepped out into the sunlight, they were met by a flurry of questions from the reporters who had gathered outside.
Microphones were thrust toward them, cameras flashed, and voices overlapped as journalists pressed for more information. "Satya, how deep does this corruption go?" one reporter shouted. "Raj, are you concerned for your safety now that you've exposed these individuals?" asked another.

Satya took a deep breath, trying to block out the noise. Raj placed a reassuring hand on her shoulder. "No comment for now," he said firmly, guiding her through the crowd. They reached their car and quickly got inside, shutting out the chaos. Satya leaned back in her seat, closing her eyes for a moment. "That was intense," she muttered. Raj nodded, turning the ignition. "Yeah, but we did it. We made sure the truth is out there."

As they drove away from the press conference, Satya's phone buzzed with messages—some from supporters, others from people she didn't recognize, offering their gratitude or asking for more details.

But one message stood out. It was from an unknown number: "You think this is over? It's just the beginning. Watch your back." Satya's heart skipped a beat. She showed the message to Raj, who frowned. "We knew there'd be threats," he said. "But we can't let them scare us." Satya nodded, but the unease settled deep within her. "What if they try to silence us?" Raj looked at her, determination in his eyes. "Then we fight harder. We've come too far to back down now."

They continued driving in silence, each of them lost in thought. Satya knew that the fight for justice wouldn't be easy, and the forces against them were powerful. But she had something they didn't—truth.
And that truth was a weapon they could not take away. As the city skyline faded into the distance, Satya made a silent vow. No matter what, she would see this through. For her grandfather. For the people who had suffered. For justice.

As they neared the outskirts of the city, Raj's phone buzzed with an incoming call. He glanced at the screen—it was

Anil, their trusted ally and the one who had helped them gather much of the evidence. "Anil, what's up?" Raj answered. "Raj, you need to get to a safe location immediately. I just got word that there's a warrant out for your arrest. They're coming for both of you," Anil's voice was urgent, laced with concern. Satya's eyes widened as she overheard the conversation. "What? How did they manage that so fast?" Raj asked, his grip tightening on the steering wheel.

"They're panicking. The evidence you revealed today hit them harder than expected. They're using their power to silence you before more comes out. I'm sending you coordinates to a safe house. Get there, and lay low for a while," Anil advised. Raj hung up and glanced at Satya. "We have no choice. We need to disappear for now." Satya nodded, "We can't just vanish, Raj. People will think we're guilty." "Right now, they control the narrative. We need to stay ahead of them and plan our next move. If we're arrested, it's over." Satya swallowed hard, knowing he was right. "Alright, let's get to the safe house."

Raj took a sharp turn, heading toward the outskirts of the city, where they could temporarily evade the authorities. As they drove, Satya's mind raced. She couldn't stop thinking about the people who were depending on them—the farmers, the workers, the families who had been cheated for so long. She couldn't let them down. They had to expose the full extent of the corruption, no matter the cost.

After what felt like hours, they reached a secluded house tucked away in the hills. Anil was already there, waiting for them. "Glad you made it," he said as they stepped inside. "What's the plan now?" Satya asked, her voice steady despite the whirlwind of emotions inside her.

"We'll lay low for a day or two while I work on getting you protection. In the meantime, we need to leak more evidence," Anil said, spreading out maps and files on a makeshift table. Satya nodded. "We need to hit them harder. We can't just play defence anymore." Raj agreed. "We expose them fully—no matter what it takes." As they plotted their next steps, the tension in the room was palpable.

They knew they were running out of time, and the powerful forces they had angered would stop at nothing to shut them down. But as the night deepened, so did their resolve. They would fight, no matter the cost. For justice. For truth. For the people who had been forgotten.

As the sun rose the next morning, Satya stared out the window, lost in thought. The air was thick with anticipation—this was the day they would make their final move. She knew once they released the last wave of evidence, there would be no going back. Anil approached with a determined look. "We've secured the right channels. The evidence will go live across multiple platforms at noon. After that, the public will know everything." Raj checked his watch. "We've only got a few hours. We need to prepare for whatever comes after." Satya turned to face them both. "We've done all we can. Now it's up to the people to decide what they do with the truth. No matter what happens, we can't let fear control us."

As noon approached, they gathered around the small table where Anil was setting up the final transmission. Satya's heart pounded, but she stood tall, knowing this was her moment. The weight of her grandfather's legacy was on her shoulders, but this time, she didn't feel crushed by it—she felt empowered.

At exactly twelve o'clock, Anil hit the send button. The data burst into the world, spreading like wildfire. Screens across the country lit up with proof of the corruption that had plagued the nation for years—names, dates, bank transactions, secret deals. Everything was out in the open now. The backlash was immediate. News stations broke into emergency broadcasts, the public erupted in outrage, and social media buzzed with demands for justice.

"We did it," Raj whispered, almost in disbelief. Satya, however, remained calm. " We may have exposed them, but the fight for change is far from over."

As the hours passed, reports came in of resignations, arrests, and protests erupting in cities across the country. The once-untouchable figures of power were now facing the consequences of their actions.
Satya knew the road ahead would still be difficult—rebuilding trust and justice would take time—but they had won the first and most important battle.

In the evening, as the sun set over the hills, Satya, Raj, and Anil stood together on the balcony of the safe house, looking out at the horizon. "This is for my grandfather," Satya whispered. "And for every person he fought for." Raj placed a hand on her shoulder. "He'd be proud of you. You've done more than you'll ever know." Satya smiled, a sense of peace settling over her.

She knew there was still much to do, but for now, they had brought light to the darkness. And in that moment, Satya knew that her grandfather would be proud if he was watching her.

CHAPTER ELEVEN

HOMECOMING OF HEARTS

Satya looked around her childhood home, now bustling with energy and laughter—so different from the lonely echoes that once filled its halls. Today was a special day. It had been years since the family had gathered under one roof. Once scattered and divided by distance, both physical and emotional, they were now united again, thanks to her. She remembered when the joint family system had broken. Her parents, aunts, and uncles had moved to different cities, caught up in their own lives, leaving behind the close-knit bond they once shared. It wasn't anyone's fault—it was just life. But deep down, Satya always missed those days when the house was filled with warmth, stories, and shared meals. But today was different. Today, they had all come back.

She had planned a family reunion and invited everyone personally to give some of their time just for a day. Everyone would again go back to their respective lives and routines but this reunion would bring back the warmth and closeness the family once had. The people who once were against her and did not want her to move forward with this case, were now extremely proud of her. She didn't want this day to be about achievements, though. This was about family—about healing old wounds and rebuilding the trust that had once bound them. Her parents stood beside her, beaming with pride.

Satya had always admired their strength, even when things got tough. She had learned so much from them—their quiet perseverance, their dedication to family, and their belief in the importance of staying connected, even when the world tried to pull them apart. Her parents were her inspiration and seeing them happy together was the thing that kept her going.

As everyone gathered around the dinner table, Satya stood to say a few words. "I want to thank you all for coming," she began, her voice steady but filled with emotion. "I know life has taken us in different directions, but today, I wanted to remind us all of something important—family is not just about living under the same roof, but about staying in each other's hearts no matter where we are. I haven't much of my time with you all except for when I used to come here in my vacations, but I always think of those times".

Her words seemed to resonate with everyone in the room. Her uncle, who had been one of the first to move away for work, nodded thoughtfully. Her cousin, who had been distant for years, smiled, understanding the significance of what Satya was trying to say.

Satya continued, "I've learned a lot from all of you. And I've learned that the values our parents taught us—the importance of respect, love, and unity—are what make us strong. We may have taken different paths, but those values are what bring us back here today."

Her mother's eyes welled up with tears, proud of the young woman her daughter had become. Satya's father placed a gentle hand on her shoulder, his silent gesture saying more than words ever could.

The day continued with laughter, stories, and shared memories. They talked about the past, but also about the future—about how they could ensure that the family would never drift apart again. They spoke of the importance of keeping traditions alive, not just for themselves but for the generations to come.

CHAPTER TWELVE

A PLACE OF REFLECTIONS

Satya sat quietly on the bed, her fingers gently tracing the edges of the worn wooden frame. The bed creaked under her weight, its legs unsteady from years of use and neglect. Her grandfather's favourite place. How many evenings had she seen him sit here, his wise eyes gazing into the distance, lost in thoughts that seemed far beyond the present?

The sunlight filtered through the old curtains, casting a soft glow over the room. Dust danced in the air, shimmering like little memories coming to life, and for a moment, Satya felt like her grandfather was still there, smiling at her with that calm, knowing expression he always had. The room had barely changed since the last time she had seen him. The small wooden table by the window still held his favourite books—pages now yellowed with time.

She thought of the wise, old, quiet man she saw in her childhood who always protected the naughty child who would run out of the house as soon as his eyes gazed off. As the years passed, her grandfather had slowly edged closer to the inevitable, his once strong presence fading like the weakening wood of the bed he sat on, until time finally took him gently from their lives. Satya closed her eyes and breathed deeply, the familiar scent of the room washing over her. It was the smell of old wood, faded ink, and something else she couldn't quite name—perhaps the remnants of a past that was slipping further away with each day.

Her grandfather had been the heart of the family, the one who always believed in the power of togetherness. It was in this room that he used to tell her stories, stories about life, courage, and family values—about how roots ran deep, and even if branches stretched far, they always found their way back to the tree. She sat still, absorbing the silence, the weight of the past pressing down on her. She could spend very less time with him.

This place had always been a sanctuary for her grandfather, a quiet corner where he could retreat from the world, reflect, and recharge. And now, it had become a sanctuary for her too. Satya's mind wandered back to her childhood, to the moments she had spent here, listening to him speak. He had always known that their family, no matter how scattered, would one day come together again. And today, after all the trials, the family had reunited, just as he had believed. They had come together, bound by the love and the strength that he had instilled in them all.

She wished he could have seen it. He would have been so proud. Tears welled up in Satya's eyes, but she didn't let them fall. Instead, she smiled. He was here, after all, in every memory, in every value he had passed down. His presence was in the laughter of her family, the unity they had found again. He was in the bond that had strengthened over time. "Thank you," she whispered softly, knowing that he could hear her wherever he was. The wooden bed creaked again as Satya stood up, but this time it sounded like a familiar old friend saying goodbye. It wasn't the same without him, but his spirit lived on in her, in the family, and in the home he had so carefully nurtured. As she walked out, closing the door gently behind her, Satya knew that this chapter of her life had come to a close, but his lessons, his love, and his strength would carry her forward forever.

Final Reflections :)

As this story comes to an end, i want to leave you with a simple message: Every journey no matter how personal, is shared with those we care about. Our family matters the most and there is nothing greater than our parents who spend most of their lives on us.

Life is filled with fleeting moments, and it's in these moments we find true meaning: whether a shared smile, a quiet reflection or the comfort of family.

May we all cherish the time we have with our loved ones and carry forward the values that unite us.

thanks a lot for reading my book.

www.ingramcontent.com/pod-product-compliance
Lightning Source LLC
Chambersburg PA
CBHW020459160726
47991CB00007B/2734